Déjà Vu: A Short Romance

Lawrence I. Hill

Published by Moody Boxfan Books, 2021.

Déjà Vu

Déjà Vu
[By Tee Mills, from the album *Peachtree Memories*]

• • • •

We grew up the same way
Playing those love games that kids play
But as I grew into a man
My feelings I could not understand
Your words had me confused
Looking in the mirror I didn't know who
Was looking back at me each day
I just knew I had to get as far away

As I could
And, baby, I did

But the distance didn't work
It just left me with the hurt
And now

Chorus:

It's like Déjà Vu
Every time I think of you
You never left my heart, why did we ever part
It's like Déjà Vu
Every time I see your face, I'm floating into space
And I don't know what to do

It's like Déjà vu

We went our separate ways
But myself I never forgave,
For not telling us the truth
Of all the things I felt for you
In my dreams I have these plans
Just want to prove myself that man
Who can finally tell you how I feel
That your smile made life feel so real

And I would
And, baby, I will

Cuz the distance didn't work
All I've got left is this hurt
And still

Chorus (x3):

It's like Déjà Vu
Every time I think of you
You never left my heart, why did we ever part
It's like Déjà Vu
Every time I see your face, I'm floating into space
And I don't know what to do
It's like Déjà vu

Ay, baby, Ay - I wonder if you ever knew
Ay, baby, Ay - that your smile was my truth
[Repeat to fade]

It's like Déjà vu

We went our separate ways
But myself I never forgave,
For not telling us the truth
Of all the things I felt for you
In my dreams I have these plans
Just want to prove myself that man
Who can finally tell you how I feel
That your smile made life feel so real

And I would
And, baby, I will

Cuz the distance didn't work
All I've got left is this hurt
And still

Chorus (x3):

It's like Déjà Vu
Every time I think of you
You never left my heart, why did we ever part
It's like Déjà Vu
Every time I see your face, I'm floating into space
And I don't know what to do
It's like Déjà vu

Ay, baby, Ay - I wonder if you ever knew
Ay, baby, Ay - that your smile was my truth
[Repeat to fade]

Déjà Vu

Déjà Vu
[By Tee Mills, from the album *Peachtree Memories*]

• • • •

We grew up the same way
Playing those love games that kids play
But as I grew into a man
My feelings I could not understand
Your words had me confused
Looking in the mirror I didn't know who
Was looking back at me each day
I just knew I had to get as far away

As I could
And, baby, I did

But the distance didn't work
It just left me with the hurt
And now

Chorus:

It's like Déjà Vu
Every time I think of you
You never left my heart, why did we ever part
It's like Déjà Vu
Every time I see your face, I'm floating into space
And I don't know what to do

CHAPTER ONE

"*D*eliciously having a wondrous wintry time....*"

The speakers in the dining room and the other main areas of the hotel where the Christmas music loop played were even louder than in the break room. It was an assault of sound.

"Ugh," Alvin exclaimed as he emerged from the break room where he'd gone to stash his coat before his shift started. "Not this damn song again!"

He ducked, just narrowly escaping being smacked in the forehead by one of the jingle bells which hung from the imitation holly garland, one of many that had been draped above each doorframe on the ground floor. "And do we really have to hang all this shit right here? This is the busiest door in the whole place. Someone's going to lose an eye, I promise."

"Oh, you sound like such a Scrooge!" objected Deniece, who stood nearby at the bar. "I could listen to this music all year long. I absolutely *love* Christmas!"

"That's worrying," intoned Alvin dryly. Although Deniece worked for him, they had become quite close, and their friendship allowed for goading and sarcasm. "As is this outfit. Dee, what *are* you wearing?"

"You know I like to dress for the holidays. I've been wearing green and red every day for the past two weeks."

"I assure you, we all noticed," said Alvin. "But this is just extra."

Deniece looked down at her outfit, which included green slacks, a garish sweater with every symbol of Christmas ever known knitted into its design, and a bunch of holly, complete with waxy red berries, pinned beside her name tag. She adjusted the Santa cap on her head and spread out her hands.

"Tomorrow is Christmas Eve, Alvin. You know we have our annual ugly sweater contest today. Remember, you have to cast your vote in the employee suggestion box before you clock out today. The winner gets a hundred dollar gift card next week as the prize, and I need that hundred bucks."

"I will do my best to remember to cast my vote. But, umm, I'm pretty sure you are going to win this contest by a landslide."

"I know you're being shady, but thank you anyway," said Deniece. "If I win, I'll make sure to get you a copy of whatever compilation CD they've been playing here."

"Don't you dare," Alvin declared. "It's not that I hate Christmas music in general; I don't. But this song—this song right here—what can I say? I have been traumatized by it."

"Well, I'm traumatized by the whole mess," declared Davon. He sauntered up to the bar, dropped his server's tray onto the polished surface, and propped one hand on his hip. "I wish they would put something a little more soulful into the mix. If I hear one more hillbilly honky-tonk ho-ho-ho, I may cry. I don't think they've updated this playlist in at least twenty-five years."

Deniece was just a few years younger than Alvin, still in school but pursuing her graduate degree at Emory. Davon was a bit older than both of them, in his mid-forties, and it felt as if he had been with the hotel since they laid the foundation. But he was a terrific server and devoted to his job at the Highstone Hotel—and he was also entertaining as hell. The dining room fell under Alvin's purview as Hospitality and Events Director, and he secretly loved whenever his shift overlapped with Davon's.

"Well, I'm all right with it. Why do you hate this song in particular, Alvin?" Deniece asked. "Did you not get the Barbie doll you wanted as a kid and it reminds you of your utter disappointment?"

"I wish," said Alvin. "No, one of my first jobs in high school, I worked at Crazy 4 Toys—that huge toy store that went out of business—and I was still working there when Christmas season hit.

"During the week of Christmas we got stuck on ten, eleven, twelve-hour shifts behind the register. Normally when it was time for our break, we had to lock or cash out our register so accounting could take it back to the office. But the Christmas shoppers were so non-stop, that during that last week, somebody would just tap us on the shoulder at the end of our shift and step right into our spot, usually mid-transaction and keeping ringing up toys. I'd never seen anything like it."

"I'm so glad I decided not to have kids, after all," said Davon. Alvin and Deniece both gave him a look. Davon cocked his head. "I don't know why y'all are gagging at me like that!"

"Anyway," Alvin continued, "they had a loop of songs, just like here, which played over and over for weeks. Then about two days before Christmas, just when I was starting my twelve-hour shift, the loop got stuck! On this one song! And it played over and over for hours on end. It was hell, I swear. I had never really liked the song to begin with, but by the end of the day, I swore if I ever heard it again, I would end my life."

"Okay, yeah, that I get," agreed Deniece.

"Well, don't do anything crazy today," Davon commanded, "we just got new floors in the break room and I don't wanna be mopping up your blood or anything. I need the overtime, but not that much."

"I'll try to curb my self-harm," said Alvin.

"Y'all are really killing my jolly Christmas vibe with all this talk." Deniece frowned. "It's my favorite season, and I'm not going to let you Grinches kill my excitement. The only thing that could make it better would be some snow. I wish I could spend every Christmas in a log cabin with the snow three feet high outside, a fire blazing, and a glass of mulled wine in my hand."

"You're going to have to get far away from Atlanta if you want all of that, Dee," said Alvin.

"I plan to. Once I'm done with school, I plan to go somewhere entirely new, Chicago or New York or maybe even London. I need to see more of the world. "

Alvin looked at her thoughtfully for a moment. "Good for you."

"Oh, please, Miss Hallmark Log Cabin," said Davon. "You know the only reason you love winter so much is because it's cuffing season. You just want to trap a man in that snowdrift fantasy of yours, that's all."

Deniece cut her eye at him. "Don't you have a table to bus?"

"I don't bus tables, heifer, you know that. And all two of my guests are well into their meal; I've got my eye on them. Don't change the subject."

"The subject was Christmas—you're the one who changed it."

"Uh huh. But what about that lawyer you were dating?" Davon affected a regal tone. "*Neil Larchmont, DDS.* Have you broken up with him yet?"

"JD, fool. He's a lawyer not a dentist. And nothing happened to him, we're still dating. Everything is fine, routine almost."

"So should we cross become a lawyer's wife off your Christmas list?" Davon asked.

"Being anybody's wife is nowhere on my list—Christmas or otherwise. I will be my own person, maybe with a husband or maybe not. I'm still figuring things out. But I may be settled down by the time I'm as old as you are."

"I'm not too old to fight you," Davon reminded her.

"Anyway. To be honest, I just haven't been feeling Neil lately. And I think it's a mutual feeling. There's just something about his smile."

"Too bad he's not a dentist, maybe he could fix that," added Davon.

"You know what," Deniece said warningly, pointing at him. "There's nothing wrong with his smile cosmetically. It just doesn't feel genuine; it's like he's only putting it on to seem happy but he doesn't really mean it. I think we're just both waiting for the better thing to come along. Until then, it's sort of just a pleasant stasis."

Alvin nodded thoughtfully.

"Yeah, yeah," said Davon. "That's great, Oprah, thank you for the intimate portrait. But I was talking about those igloo shenanigans. No repeat performance this year?"

"'Igloo shenanigans'?" Alvin asked, finally getting a word in.

"It wasn't shenanigans. Neil took me to this rooftop ice-skating venue downtown last year. And you could rent these little private cabins that were made to look like igloos. He got one for us. It was so romantic; just like my log cabin fantasy. We had hot chocolate and s'mores and just cuddled together."

"Child, and then they melted the walls right on down!" Davon cackled.

"We did no such thing, Davon. All we did was kiss and cuddle. It was really very sweet."

Alvin smiled and opened his mouth to reply but Davon was too quick.

"Sweet, huh? I bet. So all you did was 'kiss and cuddle'? And now you're telling us he isn't much interested in sex these days? He sounds a little suspect to me."

"Oh, you think everybody is gay or in the closet, Davon."

Davon sucked his teeth and was about to retort when Alvin jumped in.

"That sounds really nice, Dee, seriously. I'd love to have a night like that with someone."

"How? You're vegan. Do you even drink hot chocolate?" asked Davon.

"As long as it's made with nut milk or something. And there are vegan marshmallows, you know."

Davon scrunched up his face and gave Alvin a disdainful look.

"Vegan marshmallows? Just taking all the joy out of Christmas," he said. "Maybe you are a Scrooge. Oh, one of my tables is waving at me, I'll be right back. Save any important gossip for my return."

Alvin and Deniece moved to the end of the bar as Alvin began his start-of-shift ritual. He pulled up the reservations screen on the kiosk there.

"Who's on shift with you tonight for the dinner rush?"

"Paula, she'll be in after Davon."

"Good, Paula's as good as you. And we got a full stack of guests tonight."

"I saw," agreed Deniece, nodding. "Which reminds me! That reservation you were asking me to keep an eye out for. They checked in a couple of hours ago, before you got here. It was a celebrity alias check-in, just like you suspected. But you'll never believe who it really is!"

"Who?" asked Alvin.

"Tee Mills! Can you believe it?"

Alvin felt as if someone had punched him in the gut. He inhaled deeply, trying to catch his breath.

"I couldn't believe my eyes," Deniece continued. "He is from Atlanta though, I remember reading somewhere. So I guess he has family down here to visit for the holiday."

"Tee Mills?" Alvin repeated, his voice soft.

"Yes! I used to have such a crush on him back in the day." Deniece began to snap her fingers and sway her hips. "*Let the sheets fall where they maaaay,*" she sang, "*Cuz baby we're gonna turn night into daaay...* That was my song!"

"Must you?" asked Davon, who reappeared. "I was just trying to sell my table on the dessert menu, but they heard your caterwauling all the way over there and I assumed it turned their stomachs."

Denise sang another line at the top of her lungs.

"Please spare us, Lord!" Davon cried, covering his ears.

Alvin sighed, grateful for Davon's distraction. He didn't want to talk about Tee Mills just yet. He turned back to the screen and pretended to scroll through the schedule.

"Whatever! I can sing!" said Deniece.

"Girl, you hit the key less often than a gap-toothed piano. Don't try it."

"Nobody likes you, Davon."

"What are y'all talking about anyway?" Davon asked, ignoring Deniece.

"Tee Mills," she said.

"The singer?" asked Davon. "Who sings those freaky songs? What do you know about that kind of music, Miss Ivy League?"

"You don't know me, Davon. I distinctly remember when that song 'Night into Day' came out in my freshman year because I played it constantly. You know," she added conspiratorially, "I even lost my virginity to that album."

"Okay, that's TMI for the dining room, y'all," declared Alvin, finally finding his voice.

"What a minute." Davon furrowed his brows. "Are you telling us you didn't lose your virginity until college? You actually waited that long?"

"Yes. Is that so hard to believe?"

"Well, Moses parted the Red Sea, so, honey, I guess unbelievable things happen all the time."

"Ugh. I hate you entirely and completely."

Alvin turned around. "You know, you two sound just like brother and sister."

"Gross," they responded in unison.

Davon studied Alvin for a moment. "What inspired this reminiscing anyway?"

Alvin punched a few more commands on the screen. "It doesn't matter. We should get to work."

"Not just yet," said Davon. "Something's not right. I know her singing was soul-shakingly terrible but—"

"Shut up, Davon," Deniece interjected.

"But, Alvin, you look like somebody slapped you," Davon continued, unfazed.

"No, it's not her singing. Or anything. I'm just surprised, that's all. I thought it might be him, but I wasn't sure."

"Might be who?"

"Tee Mills, like I just said," said Deniece. "He's the celebrity booking from earlier today. He's booked into the presidential suite."

"Is that all? I know you can't be nervous about a celebrity booking, Alvin, we get them all the time."

"I just didn't expect this particular celebrity guest; that's all."

"What's wrong with Tee Mills?"

"Nothing's wrong with him, I just haven't seen him in a long time. And we weren't the best of friends even then."

Deniece was invested now. "Wait, hold up. 'Friends'? What are you talking about? How were you and Tee Mills friends?"

"We went to school together."

She smacked his arm. "No, you did not. Stop lying!"

"I'm not lying. Franklin Schofield—the name on the reservation? That was my school. Franklin Schofield Junior High. That's why it stuck out to me when we first noticed it. Tee Mills and I met in junior high and then went to high school together."

"I remember that Schofield place." Davon drummed his fingers against his tray. "It was that private Catholic school."

"Y'all were Catholic?" Deniece was surprised.

"No, not at all," said Alvin. "Our parents just sent us there because they thought that's where we'd get the best education."

"Wasn't that the place that they shut down years ago?" asked Davon. "Because the principal and the vice-principal were having an affair and stealing all the school donations?"

"Yeah, that's the place," said Alvin.

Deniece gasped and Davon continued.

"I thought so! It was quite the *escándalo,* honey! The principal did some time for it too. Luckily, the vice-principal's husband was a lawyer so he got her off. They divorced a couple years later if I remember correctly."

"You seem to remember a lot of things quite correctly," Alvin said with a pointed look. "Anyway, Tim—sorry, Tee Mills–and I were kinda sorta friends back in those days. Up until ninth grade, at least, when we both transferred to the public high school. There were so many more students there. And the pressure to, you know, fit in, and find your clique was greater too so we kind of drifted apart after that."

Davon crossed his arms. "You mean he couldn't hang around the little gay boy anymore—he had to prove how butch and normal he was."

Alvin felt his face flush. "I didn't say all of that."

"Typical closet queen."

"Tee Mills isn't gay!" Denise interrupted.

"Hmph," Davon replied. "I know what I know. He's very suspect."

"Here you go again," said Deniece, exasperated. "Thinking that everybody is gay."

"No. Just the gay ones. The tea on the streets is that he's family."

"'Family'?" Deniece asked.

Davon rolled his eyes. "One of the children, of a certain persuasion, a ho-mo-sexual— Girl, how long have you been friends with us? Pick up the lingo, bitch."

"Look." Deniece raised a finger. "I've told you about calling me a bitch."

Alvin jumped in to deescalate. "And when you say 'the streets' do you mean those trashy blogs you read?" asked Alvin.

"Don't you dare judge me, you uppity strumpet," Davon cried. "I'll have you know that *The Shady Corner* is a reputable journalistic establishment. They broke the news about the new cast of *The Actual Homemakers of Poughkeepsie* months before anybody else and they also knew that Cherylla had had a baby and her lips done too during the hiatus. Tell me that's not investigative journalism."

Neither Deniece nor Alvin had a response to that.

"Anyway." Davon spread his hand out. "Back to your high school hookups."

"He was not my hookup," Alvin insisted. "We were just friends, like I said, and barely even that."

"I'm not sure I buy it." Deniece cocked her head. "If y'all really went to school together, then why would you be so bothered that he was simply staying as a guest?"

"Did I say I was bothered?"

"You sure looked bothered," Deniece said. "And, another thing, why didn't you keep in touch? I know if I had a millions-of-albums-selling-friend who I'd known from childhood, I'd at least make sure we stayed in touch. You were quick to guess he was registered under that pseudonym, so it doesn't seem too far from your mind."

"Pshaw! I don't know what you mean by that. I recognized the name, that's it. And, as for keeping in touch, we didn't exactly run in the same circles in high school."

"No, you don't say!" Deniece feigned disbelief. "Oh wow. That's such a surprise. Imagine the fine-ass kid who would later go on to be one of the biggest R&B singers on the planet and the nerdy-ass dude who went on to be the supervisor of... this place..." She waved dismissively at the dining room. "Not remaining bosom buddies."

"I might just be a Hospitality and Events Director but I am still *your* supervisor if I need to remind you. And none of this is a big deal, okay? We just went to high school together!"

"Well, now's your chance for a grand reunion."

All three jumped a little and turned to see the general manager, Mister Randall, standing there.

"Oh, look, I just noticed that my table is waving at me." Davon grabbed his tray and quickly moved off.

Alvin cleared his throat. "Mister Randall, sorry, I didn't see you there."

"Yes, I got that impression," said Randall. "This celebrity booking, I need you to get up to his suite and handle some requests his team has. They're going to be doing interviews in the suite all afternoon so he needs some provisions and a special setup."

"I've just clocked in, Mister Randall, and I've still got my rounds to make. Maybe Deniece could handle this request?"

Deniece put on her best smile and nodded.

"Sure, Deniece, why don't you help him? You could use the training anyway."

Deniece's smile faltered.

"I'm sure she could handle it by herself," Alvin insisted.

Randall shook his head. "Nope, sorry. The client especially requested you. So this one is yours to handle."

Deniece's eyes went wide.

"Chop-chop." Randall turned to leave. "This is a high-profile client; we need to keep him happy. They're expecting you upstairs within fifteen minutes."

Alvin swallowed hard and dashed through the door beside the bar and back into the break room. Inside, he just stood in the middle of the room, as if adrift. Seconds later he was followed by Deniece and then Davon.

"Did I hear him say 'special request'?" asked Davon as the door swung shut behind them.

"Oh wow, I guess you really were friends," Deniece added.

"I'm not friends with that asshole," said Alvin sharply. He gripped the back of a nearby chair and leaned into it, his chest moving in and out.

Deniece and Davon exchanged a glance.

"Are you okay?" Deniece asked. "This has really gotten to you. When you were kids did this Tee Mills guy bully you back then?"

Alvin closed his eyes and shook his head. He took a deep breath. "I wouldn't go so far as to call him a bully, but he did constantly give me a hard time. Along with his friends. When we were at school, at least. All three of us."

"All three of you?" asked Davon.

"Yeah, me and my best friends, Teddy and Simone." Alvin turned to face them and leaned against the chair. "We were our own little group—of outsiders, I guess. We never really fit in with most of the other kids; they kept their distance, as if they all knew."

"That y'all were all gay?" offered Davon.

Alvin nodded.

"And a little bit nerdy," he continued. "And a little bit alternative. And just—well, not good for blending into a high school in general. Tim and his friends constantly teased us. They called us Alvin, Simon, and Theodore."

Deniece put her hand to her mouth. "You mean, like the Chipmunks?"

She tried to stifle a laugh but when Davon burst out cackling, she followed suit.

"Oh, that's nice," said Alvin, shaking his head. "Fuck y'all very much."

"I'm sorry." Deniece bit her lip. "But did you have the glasses and everything?"

"Simon was the one with the glasses, Deniece, not Alvin." He looked at his fingernails. "But yes, yes, I did."

"Oh, poor baby," said Davon.

"Anyway!" Alvin declared loudly, straightening. "Come on, Deniece, his majesty awaits upstairs. And I have to handle this, you heard the boss."

As Alvin and Deniece left the room Davon, waving his fist in the air, bellowed behind them, "Allllllviiiiin!"

Alvin shook his head, calling back, "Nobody likes you, Davon."

"See," cried Deniece, turning back to Davon to stick out her tongue, "I told you!"

CHAPTER TWO

"**M**otherfucking ever-loving Christ, Ladonna, I told you no fucking fedoras!"

The door to the suite was flung open to reveal a middle-aged woman flinging epithets back into the room, her full, curly hair, dyed flame-red, and her cat's-eye glasses threatening at any moment to leap off her animated face.

"Yes?" she asked by way of greeting to Alvin and Deniece.

"We're here from management," declared Alvin.

"Oh, thank Christ! Please, come in, come in."

She waved, ushering them into the living room area of the suite.

"I'm Angie, his manager," she said as she snatched a sheet of paper from a nearby table. She pressed it into Alvin's hand. "Here's the rider with a list of stuff we'll need for the interview sessions this afternoon. We start in an hour and forty-seven minutes. So please make sure this stuff is here fifteen minutes before that. At the latest! Oh, and please get him whatever he needs too. I don't need him complaining midway through about his stomach grumbling or that it's been three hours since his last protein fix or any of that shit. If you've got any of those nutrition bars—you know the ones—add, like, a dozen to the list. If he doesn't eat them, I can always use them to pummel the paparazzi." She grabbed her bag, fished out a packet of cigarettes and pulled one out with her mouth, poised to be lit. "Now, I'm going downstairs. I just need an hour in the pool or the hot tub."

"Our pool is closed right now," said Dee apologetically. "Out of season. And the hot tub doesn't open until six o'clock."

"You've gotta be fucking kidding me. But you're at least serving cocktails now, right? Or is this one of those Bible states?"

"Of course," answered Alvin. "Cocktails are always available at our seated bar."

"Thank Christ. That's all I need."

"We have a special Candy Alexander Seasonal Cocktail, in fact," added Deniece. "It's made with Bailey's, crème de cacao, a splash of peppermint schnapps and it comes garnished with candy cane dust."

Angie recoiled in disgust.

"Were you drinking one of those when you picked out that sweater, hon?" she asked.

Deniece's mouth fell open.

Angie peered over their shoulders. "Tee!" she called out. "Tee! Get out here. The hotel people are here!" She looked over at one of the nearby stylists. "Make sure he's ready in an hour with three different changes. Quick ones, so we can do them between junkets. And no fucking crazy patterns, this time, I've told you about that shit. No Christmas, no Kwanzaa, no Hanukkah. It may be the season, but he wants to look sleek and stylish not like a parade float. Sorry, no offense, hon." She added to Deniece. "Oh, and Ladonna, I swear to God, if you try any crazy shit with hats or nose rings or chokers or any of that fucking Erykah Badu shit you love, I'm snatching you bald and cancelling your 401k, you hear me?"

The woman nearest them, presumably Ladonna, pursed her lips and rolled her eyes, but nodded.

"All right, I'm out," Angie announced, and whooshed out of the door.

Dee turned to Alvin and widened her eyes. "Wow."

"Ang!"

They heard a voice behind them and turned around.

"Hey, Ang? You still here?"

Tee Mills emerged from the bedroom, and all the air left Alvin's lungs.

"Daaaaaamn," Deniece said under her breath. Alvin silently co-signed.

Tee Mills was wearing nothing but a skin-tight pair of briefs that barely seemed to contain all of him, and a chain around his neck. There was a bauble at the end of the chain, but when Tee Mills saw them there, he grasped it and flung it around so that the bauble fell over his back. His eyes met Alvin's from across the room and he went silent, their gazes locked.

He was breathtaking in his beauty. As he always had been, thought Alvin. He stood there in his six-foot-plus glory, his former high school track star body morphed into an ode to perfection. His skin was luminous and radiant, glowing with health and the most expensive products one could buy. How many times, Alvin wondered, had he imagined that skin, velvety brown like his, under his fingertips, touched by his lips, pressing against him in a tight embrace? High-paid celebrity trainers and a micro-managed diet had chiseled him into an artist's rendering of manliness. His broad shoulders, tapered waist, thick thighs, and, Alvin cleared his throat as Tee Mills turned to his side to grab a shirt thrown over a nearby chair, his deliciously round ass.

"Ang, I think we're gonna have to cut the last interview."

Tee Mills seemed to make a show of studying the shirt.

"Angie left," Alvin replied, his tone flat.

Tee Mills looked at him again. Again, that same moment of eyes locking, but he said nothing. The silence felt awkward and seemed to stretch on.

Deniece broke it by saying, "Hi, Mister Mills, we're here to get you set up for this afternoon. Your manager said there might be some things you need."

Tee Mills didn't respond, he just held Alvin's gaze.

Alvin folded his hands in front of him. "Yeah. We're the 'hotel people.'"

He could feel Deniece giving him a hard side-eye but he ignored it.

Tee Mills pushed his focus over to the couch, where outfits had been laid out for his perusal. He started asking questions about the clothes, no longer acknowledging the presence of Alvin or Deniece. He asked Ladonna a question about a specific piece.

"It's over there," Ladonna replied, pointing in the general direction of where Alvin and Deniece waited.

Tee Mills meandered over, squeezing between them. Alvin felt like stone and though he knew he should step aside, he wasn't able to move. Deniece, however, complied.

"Pardon me, beautiful," Tee Mills said to her, his voice deep and seductive.

As he came close Alvin could smell cocoa butter, vanilla, a hint of citrus, and something spicy from his cologne. He had to will himself not to lean in close and inhale deeply of the scent. He was annoyed with himself at the depth of his want.

"That's okay." Dee practically giggled in response.

Alvin gave her a hard look.

"What?" she mouthed at him.

For several minutes more, Tee Mills shuffled through accessories and other wardrobe pieces behind them, only exchanging occasional words with Ladonna and the stylists.

Deniece pursed her lips and shrugged at Alvin as they waited in silence.

"Well, Mister Mills, if you don't need anything." Alvin stalked toward the door, Deniece trotted after.

"Wait!" Tee Mills called out with surprising force. He approached them, fiddling with the chain around his neck. He cleared his throat, and examined his nails as he asked, "Is there any way you can get me something to eat too?"

"Of course, anything in particular?" Alvin replied, his voice the height of politeness.

Tee Mills looked up at him and their eyes met. Something flashed across his expression, a ferocity that Alvin felt directed toward him, and for a brief moment he felt a stirring in his stomach.

"I'm not picky, I'm just starving." He rubbed his hand across his chiseled abs. "Maybe, like, a burger? Grass-fed, lean. And no bun, I'm off carbs right now. And dairy."

Alvin nodded. "Of course, Mister Mills."

"Thanks," Tee Mills said, a small smile forming on his lips. He cocked his head and gave Alvin that look again. "And you can call me Tee."

Alvin turned his attention to the paper which Angie had shoved into his hands earlier and folded it in half. As he pressed the fold into a crease without taking his eyes from it, he replied. "Of course, Mister Mills. We'll have that burger sent right up, along with all of your other requests."

And he turned then and opened the door without a glance back.

"It was nice to meet you, Tee Mills." Deniece's voice was girlish and high. "You don't think that maybe later I could get an autograph or something? It's for my little cousin, of course, not me, it's just that she's a huge fan of yours."

Alvin gripped the door handle. His jaw was set in a hard line as he stared at the electric candles placed in a nearby alcove for decoration.

"Deniece!"

"Here I come," she replied. "Thank you so much, Mister Mills. Oh, and I like your chain. Thanks again. Okay. Goodbye. See you later."

Out in the hallway, Alvin gave her the once-over.

"Have you fully recovered?" he asked dryly.

"Anyway!" she replied and skipped towards the elevator.

• • • •

RIDING DOWN, DENIECE studied Alvin as he leaned against the wall.

He glared at her, asking, "Do I have something on my face?"

"No," said Deniece with a sly smile. "It's just that I see now."

"See what?"

"You had a serious crush on that man in high school, that's why you didn't want to deal with him now."

"I don't know what you're talking about," Alvin snapped. Could he have been so transparent? "I told you, we weren't even really friends in high school."

"So?"

"So. So, why would I have had a crush on him? He was an asshole to me."

"Uh huh."

"I mean, you saw how he was just now. Supposedly they 'especially' asked for me, and then he didn't even acknowledge me or act like he knew who I was."

"Yeah, that was kind of shady."

The elevator came to a stop and they headed for the kitchen.

Alvin shrugged as they walked, reaching for logic. "Maybe they didn't actually request me by name but just as a director or something."

"No," said Deniece, "there are much more important people on shift right now." He cut his eye at her. "I'm just saying! There are. It must have been you specifically."

"But why would he do that and then not even speak to me?"

Deniece shook her head. "Maybe he wanted to flex. To show an old school friend how far he's come since then."

"He's a worldwide star; he didn't need to remind me of that. His face is everywhere."

"You know these celebrity types. They always have ego issues. For all his showing off his body and preening, he's probably deeply insecure."

"It didn't seem like that, walking around the room half-naked, without a care."

Deniece sighed heavily as they pushed open the swinging doors into the kitchen.

"Maybe he wanted to show you what you were missing, see if it sparked any interest."

"That doesn't make any sense," said Alvin. "He could have anybody he wants, why would he be interested in me? I'm not exactly a catch, as y'all keep reminding me. Not for someone like him, that is. Besides, we don't even know that he's not straight, no matter what Davon says."

"What Davon knows!" a voice called out.

Davon sat on a stool to one side of the kitchen, in a small area where the cooks took their meal breaks. He usually took his comp meal there at the end of his shift, to escape the dining room, and also because he was friendly with the cooks and they always gave him generous portions which he did not want Randall or anybody else to notice.

"Y'all can doubt me all you want," he continued. "I know what I know. And if he does like his tea extra-sweet, and you're too scared to take a sip, make sure you give him my number." Davon smiled a wicked smile.

"I'm not giving him your number," said Alvin.

"At least my Instagram handle. My Twitter? Something. I don't mind sliding into those DMs, baby."

Deniece waved, dismissing this talk. "What I'm trying to tell you, Alvin, is that you don't have any reason to be self-conscious now. You're not that nerdy kid with glasses anymore. You've got a lot going for you; you're smart, you're successful. You've grown into a very attractive man. You are a catch, no matter what jokes we throw at you."

"Don't do it, Dee-Dee! Don't flirt with your boss, honey. We both know that bicycle ain't built for two!"

"Shut up, Davon," Alvin and Deniece responded in unison.

"I'm just saying," she continued. "You're not that little kid anymore. You're so much more now. Show him the new and improved you."

"This is giving me Sandy in *Grease* teas," said Davon.

Deniece smiled. "You mean like the shy librarian who takes off her glasses, shakes out her hair, and suddenly she's hot?"

Davon pointed at Deniece, jabbing the air with a steak fry for emphasis. "Very much that!"

"Look, this little narrative y'all are constructing is cute, but Tee Mills is not checking for me."

Alvin hoped that ended the discussion as he turned away from them. He couldn't let himself get lost in those fantasies yet again. They had consumed his young mind. He had run all the way from Atlanta to California to get as far away from those memories of Tim as he could.

"The past is the past, Alvin. You can't worry about that. So what if he was your high school crush? You're both grown-ass men now."

Alvin gritted his teeth. "For the last time, he was not my high school crush."

"Tell a lie and shame the devil!" Davon shouted.

Alvin spun around, his tone biting. "Don't you need to run home and get ready to go troll the clubs for trade, sis?" He snarled the last word with an exaggerated hiss.

Davon's mouth fell open. "That was uncalled for." He snatched up his silverware, laid it on the side of his plate, and lifted it and his glass of iced tea. "I think I'll finish my dinner at the bar."

"Davon—" Alvin started, feeling abashed.

"Nope! No, thank you!" Davon called waspishly.

As he turned to his side to push out the swinging doors, he looked down his nose at Alvin.

"And besides, bitch, it's only mid-afternoon and you know I never show up to the club until at least eleven o'clock."

Alvin ran his hands across his face and massaged his temples. "We've wasted way too much of the afternoon on all this mess," he said. "I don't have time for it. I'll speak with the kitchen about the special requests. Dee, if you could please make sure they get up to the room as soon as they're ready. I have that wedding reception in the grand banquet hall starting in a couple of hours and I really need to concentrate on that."

"Got it, Mister Hospitality and Events Director," she answered with a small curtsy.

"Don't start, Dee. " He headed to the back to find the kitchen manager. He paused to smile at her. "And thank you, by the way."

• • • •

ALVIN GAZED ACROSS the room at the loving couple, trying not to be sick at the sight of them. A flush of irritation washed over him and he turned up his megawatt Hospitality and Events Director smile until he thought his face might crack. Newly married and flush with champagne, they were well into the get-down portion of the celebration. Their first sweet, loving dance had finished and the tempo had picked up. He eyed the group of bridesmaids huddled at the side of the dance floor, just waiting for the couple to finish their gyrations and the big beat drop in the song they could all pounce in.

Alvin eyed the flutes of Dom Perignon and Prosecco in their hands as they twirled their arms and flailed excitedly to the music. He smiled to himself, thinking of how Davon always insisted it was the ones who chose Prosecco at the open bar who always caused the biggest scene, while Deniece warned them to be careful of anybody who abandoned the champs for cocktails or brown liquor.

It was a relief to smile an honest smile. Most of the time he enjoyed wedding-related functions at the hotel, they were his favorite events to coordinate. But not today. He couldn't shake the uneasiness seeing Tim again had stirred up. And though the celebrity's suite was floors and floors above him, the knowledge of his presence even that close hovered over the afternoon like a specter.

A sweet-faced lady for whom makeup was obviously only an occasional voyage outside of still waters approached him, smiling. She held a flute in each hand. As she approached him, he recognized her as the mother of the bride whom he'd met on several occasions.

"Excuse me, darling, but you work here, don't you?"

"Yes, ma'am."

"Good, I just wanted to check about the buffet," she said, pointing at the long tables of food that had been set up. This couple had chosen to start their reception with their first dance and people were eating throughout the night, when the mood struck them, instead of a formal seated affair.

"Yes, ma'am, how can I help you?"

"My daughter told me—my single daughter, not the one over there shaking her tail–told me that some of the guests were *veejehtarians* or whatever they call them."

"Yes, ma'am."

"She says we talked about it with that young man who was arranging the food, but it doesn't look like there's anything for them to eat."

Alvin lifted his chin and straightened his spine. "Yes ma'am, Mrs. Ferguson. I'm the one who arranged the buffet. You and I met on several occasions."

"Oh did we?" Mrs. Ferguson looked flustered. "I am so sorry." She held up a glass. "Blame it on the bubbly, I reckon."

"Yes, ma'am," he said flatly.

"So you say we've got something they can eat then?"

"If you'll allow me," Alvin began, reaching for the flutes. He took one from each hand and set them down on a nearby table. He held out his arm. "I'll be happy to show you."

He led her to the portion of the buffet which contained the vegan options. He showed her the various dishes and explained each one, trying not to let his voice sound as if he were talking to a child.

"Really? So they can eat all this here?" Mrs. Ferguson asked in disbelief.

"Yes, ma'am."

"But it doesn't look like only vegetables. It actually looks good."

Alvin's eyes narrowed but he tried not to let her see any change in his demeanor.

"Let me make you a little sample," he insisted.

He put together a tasting plate with a good bit of the best options and handed it to her. She sniffed the plate, which caused him to wince, and that he did not hide. She picked up a small veggie tart and stuck out her tongue, letting it only touch the edge. She reminded Alvin of some strange salamander or lizard he might have seen on a nature documentary.

"It won't hurt you, ma'am, I assure you."

She didn't look as if she entirely believed him but took a small bite.

"Well, I'll be damned," she declared. "That's delicious."

"Thank you," said Alvin. "Now try that."

She followed his instructions as to tasting order and even finished with one of the mini coconut milk mousse dessert cups.

"Ain't that something?" She dusted the crumbs from her fingers. "That tasted like regular food. Like good eating, in fact!"

"Thank you, ma'am. They're my own recipes."

"Your recipes?" She looked at him in disbelief. "Are you the cook, too?"

He smiled his megawatt Director smile. "No, ma'am. But I am trained as a chef. I trained in California, at some of the best culinary institutions after I left college, and worked there for some years. Our in-house Chef, Chef Michel, is amazing, but vegan cooking is not his specialty. So I've collaborated with him to make sure our menu is inclusive."

Mrs. Ferguson patted his arm. "If you can cook like that, why the hell are you working in this place? You should open a restaurant."

Alvin nodded. "I did, briefly. When I first moved back to Atlanta. But it didn't last."

Mrs. Ferguson huffed. "I bet not. Some of the folks around here ain't the most sophisticated bunch sometimes."

You don't say, Miss Lizard Tongue, Alvin thought but refrained from saying.

"Seems like California would've been a better place for you," she continued.

"There's nothing wrong with Atlanta," he replied, feeling the need to defend his hometown.

But, in truth, it was a thought Alvin had had himself for years. Atlanta was a lovely place to live, yet there was something in him that felt off-center, out-of-place. The things he came looking for when he moved back – whatever they were exactly – were not here to be found. So why was he still here? He couldn't say.

He had moved back to Atlanta to help his parents when they got into a terrible car accident. His sister had been newly married with twins and a job and she couldn't do it all. He insisted he was glad to help, and that his stay would only be temporary until they were on their feet again. But that didn't take as long as expected, and he'd felt even less needed when his parents had decided to sell their house. Life was too short, they'd decided, to waste money and time on a big mortgage and an even bigger yard. The time and money they saved living in an apartment allowed them to pour themselves into travel. They had made it a mission to see the world. Meanwhile, his sister and her husband were rocketing to star roles in their jobs, and had taken up their own big mortgage and even bigger yard in the nicest part of Vinings.

Everybody seemed to have carved out a new space in life, except him. So he'd tried his hand at his dream of opening a restaurant. And when that had flopped, he fell flat. He had learned a new lesson. Keep it tight, don't dream too big. Since then he had just been floating through his life.

"Oh good lord!" Mrs. Ferguson exclaimed, breaking him out of his reverie. "That stupid girl."

Alvin turned to look and saw that one of the bridesmaids had caught her dress on fire. They were hideous things, the bridesmaids' dresses, with lots of flounces and ruched material on the side, and in her inebriated stupor she had backed into one of the table decorations which contained a candle.

She was screeching, as were several of her friends, and people were swatting at the flames, trying to dampen them.

Alvin glanced at the buffet, snatched a bottle of wine from its ice bucket and dashed across the dance floor, bucket in hand. When he was close enough, he doused the young woman's lower half with the water and half-melted ice.

The flames extinguished, a little round of cheers and congratulatory chatter arose. The girl, who had just been slightly on fire, gasped. She gazed down at her wet, half-ruined dress and screwed her face up in anger.

"My shoes are soaking wet now."

Contempt filled her voice, her eyes flashing.

"You're welcome?" Alvin answered with a bemused tilt of the head.

"They cost me two hundred bucks," she snapped.

Alvin looked at her shoes and then back up to her flushed face.

"Maybe you can use what's left of your dress to dry them off then," he suggested with a hint of acid.

The woman grunted. "Now I have to go change!"

She aggressively shoved her champagne flute into his hand and stalked off, a trio of her friends tottering after.

Alvin stood there for a moment in disbelief until someone tapped on his shoulder.

"That was impressive," said the very tall, very handsome man beside him.

"Oh, thanks. Just part of the job, I guess."

"Are you responsible for this reception? I'm Paul, by the way. Friend of the bride."

"Nice to meet you, Paul. I'm Alvin. And not entirely, but I did have a hand in it. I'm Events Director here at the hotel, so I am mainly here to make sure things go smoothly and everyone's needs are met."

Paul gave him a quick once-over. "I'm sure you excel at that." He glanced over his shoulder. "I suppose that means you'll be here all evening then?"

Alvin smiled. "Yes, until the party's over."

Paul stepped a little closer.

"Great. Then maybe later we could get a drink together. If you're not too busy?"

Alvin looked at that handsome face, a face he would normally not have been able to keep his eyes off, and his stomach did a flip. But not a good flip. He had a sudden feeling of queasiness, as if he were about to do something very bad. He realized that it was guilt and apprehension. It was ridiculous but he felt as if he were about to cheat on a significant other. He chastised himself and tried to quell the feeling.

"I'm sure I won't be too busy," he said, though his tone wasn't as convincing as it should have been.

Paul didn't seem to notice. "Terrific. I was really hoping that—"

He was interrupted by the DJ taking the mic.

"All right, folks," announced the DJ. "This is a special request from the groom. One of his favorite songs, which he says always reminds him of his honey. It's a classic, y'all will remember it well: 'Déjà Vu'!"

We grew up the same way, playing those love games that kids play....

You've gotta be kidding me, thought Alvin.

But as I grew into a man...

Tee Mills' voice filled the room, his smoky baritone reverberating like the slinky electronic bassline that surrounded it.

My feelings I could not understand...

"This is a great song," said Paul, nodding. He looked at Alvin. "Are you okay, Alvin?"

Alvin blinked and shook his head. It was a little surreal, standing here, feeling this way, buffeted on all sides by that voice.

"I'm sorry.... I, um, I.... I just remembered something I need to do." Alvin searched for his words. "In the–um–in the office. S-s-sorry, I've gotta run."

"Sure. Okay. But still a yes on that drink later?" asked Paul.

"Yeah, yeah, of course. Sorry, I've just gotta..."

Alvin turned abruptly and made his way quickly out of the reception hall.

Once in the hallway, he looked around, feeling frantic. Seeing an outside door, he dashed for it.

It was night now, and had gone quite chilly, so he found himself alone on the outside lounge patio and was glad of it. He pulled at the collar of his suit, and leaned against the wall, inhaling the cold air. It filled his lungs and went a way to calming his anxiety. He bent over, grasping his kneecaps until he felt his head was clear again.

"Get it together, Alvin," he chastised himself.

The sooner this shift was over and he could get out of this hotel and away from the Ghost of Lost Loves Past upstairs, the sooner he would feel normal again. He had not been this shaken up in quite some time, and it was not a feeling he enjoyed.

He wrung his hands and straightened. Perhaps he would get somebody else in Hospitality and Events to handle what remained of this reception. It wasn't that he now wanted to avoid Paul for the rest of the evening, but it wouldn't have been a bad thing either, he told himself. Besides, he had plenty of boring paperwork waiting in his office to occupy his mind for the rest of the night.

· · · ·

ALVIN LOOKED DOWN AT his plate.

It was late and the bar and dining room had cleared out. At some point they had switched the music rotation into something a little less grating on his frayed nerves. Just now a smooth jazz version of a classic carol was drifting around the dining room. Normally he might have groaned at the cheesy instrumentation, but tonight he liked the familiarity of it. The string lights twinkled all along the edges of the room, now dimmed for the evening, and it felt cozy and almost slightly magical. It was nice having the place virtually to himself. It felt safe and he had made sure he was ensconced in the corner with his meal.

He pushed the food around his plate with a fork. It was his favorite comfort food dish—one of the ones he'd shown Chef Michel how to make. Chicken of the woods mushrooms, fried and smothered in gravy, and served with farro and sweet potato mash. Even Chef Michel, a committed carnivore, had to admit to liking this one. But Alvin had no appetite.

He signaled to the bartender, Sylvia, who refilled his glass of red wine.

"Hey, we have a dessert order for you to take up," said Julio, one of the cooks, coming up beside him.

"To deliver to a room?"

"Yeah."

"Have Deniece do it. I'm having dinner."

"Deniece clocked out about two hours ago. Besides, Randall says you have to do it."

Alvin sighed. "'Have to'?"

"Yup. You got your marching orders. Anyway, it's in the window. And the boss added a bottle of champagne to be a kiss-ass."

"My shift is almost over," said Alvin, irritated. "Somebody else will have to deal with it."

"No can do, partner, it's on you." Julio shrugged. "It's a special request of the celeb booking."

"Oh, come on. This bullshit again?" Alvin muttered.

Julio shrugged.

"Guess he's a real QE2. Good luck with that."

QE2 or "Queen Elizabeth the Second" was their code for high-maintenance guests, rich bookings who were always stupidly particular but had to be catered to because of the money they spent. The Highstone was the premiere high-end hotel in Atlanta and it was determined to keep its reputation.

Alvin quickly downed his glass of red and lifted his hand.

"One more, please, Sylvia."

CHAPTER THREE

Alvin knocked on the door and it opened without pause. He expected to see another frazzled assistant or some poor flunky who'd been forced onto the night shift of babysitting the grand diva, but instead it was just Tee Mills himself.

Gone was the reserved attitude of the afternoon; Tee Mills smiled at him, biting his bottom lip a little as he did. Alvin cleared his throat and tried not to notice that though his demeanor may have changed, his wardrobe hadn't much. He wore only a robe, which was open low, exposing a broad expanse of his chest. Glistening against his skin was the same chain he had been wearing earlier.

"Here you are, finally," said Tee Mills, giving Alvin a thorough once-over. "What? Service, but no smile?"

Alvin fought the urge to roll his eyes and instead painted on the fakest of smiles. "Where would you like it, sir?"

Tee Mills lifted a brow and smirked. "Over there," he indicated, stepping aside, "just inside the bedroom."

The bedroom?

"Wouldn't you prefer to take your dessert at the table there?" he suggested.

"No, thank you."

Alvin nodded and wheeled the cart inside, heading toward the bedroom. He positioned it just inside the entry and turned to leave but Tee Mills blocked the door.

Alvin cleared his throat, pulling at his jacket to smooth it. Tee Mills dipped around him and grabbed the bottle on ice waiting on the cart.

"Champagne. Perfect." He turned to Alvin. "Have a glass with me? Or maybe two? I'm free all night and I was hoping for some company."

He held the bottle in one hand, and reached down to grab himself with the other. From the tent his manhood was making, it was clear he was wearing nothing under the robe.

Alvin felt a heat at the back of his neck and he tensed, imagining what might be under that soft cloth. But he pushed those thoughts away and narrowed his eyes. "I'm sorry, sir, but it's not encouraged for staff to fraternize with the guests in such a manner. Is there anything else I can get you, Mister Miller—I'm sorry, Mister Mills?"

Tee Mills bit his lip and gave a half nod. He replaced the champagne on the cart.

"Mister Mills? So it's like that?"

"Like what?"

Alvin turned and began to leave. "If you need anything else, Mister Mills, you know how to reach us. My shift is ending shortly though, so maybe if you call down, you could ask for someone else."

Tee Mills caught up with him and grabbed him by the arm.

"Wait, Alvin."

Alvin eyed the fingers grasping him. He stared at the hand there, afraid to meet Tee Mills' gaze.

"Don't go. Please. Don't do it like this."

He looked up, anger prickling. "'Like this'? And what is this exactly? Sorry, but I don't have time for game playing. We left all that behind in school, *Timothy*. Or at least we should have." He nodded and tried to smile.

"You always had a temper, Mister Bailey. You never minced your words, that's for sure."

"I don't think this has anything to do with my temper, Mister Miller. I just don't like being played, that's all."

Tee Mills seemed surprised. "I'm not trying to play you, Alvin. But why are you acting like we're strangers?"

"Aren't we? You did a good job of acting like you didn't know who I was earlier today. You looked right through me and didn't even speak, so I took my cue from you. Just like in high school."

"Wait a minute now," said Tee hurriedly. He tightened the belt of his robe; his excitement had died down, Alvin noticed. "I'm sorry for earlier. I got nervous and I didn't know what to say exactly. But, as far as back in the day, you're the one who stopped speaking to me in high school."

Alvin shook his head in disbelief. "Are you high?"

"I might have smoked a little to take the edge off, but I'm clear-headed enough to know the truth," Tee Mills replied.

Alvin guffawed. "You've gotta be kidding, right?"

Tee Mills leaned back against the cart and crossed his arms. "How so?"

"*I* stopped talking to *you*? If that's true, I only did it because you treated me like an asshole. You stopped seeking me out to talk; you got a whole new group of friends. And even when I got that hint as a kid, and just tried to be generally friendly, you wouldn't even let me do that. I'll never forget that day you were standing with your boys by the stairwell, and as I walked up I smiled and nodded hello and you just turned the other way. Quickly. Stone-faced."

"I didn't mean—"

"Then I heard one of your boys, snickering, talking about why I was grinning like a faggot. And as I passed, you turned your whole body away and started talking to somebody else. I got the message."

"That was just one incident, Alvin. And that was a lifetime ago."

Alvin couldn't stem his annoyance. "One time? So you're saying I had other chances to allow you to prove you were still my friend? Or was I just supposed to keep humiliating myself? You were cold and ignored me at every turn—just like this afternoon. When people were around, I wasn't to be acknowledged."

Tee Mills fingered the chain around his neck. "You got your own group of friends too, you know. You didn't have anything to do with me anymore either."

"Alvin, Simon, and Theodore?" Tee dropped his eyes, clearly embarrassed. "Yeah. I remember y'all's little nickname for us. They were actual friends. But we got tired of being made fun of, so I kept away from people like you."

Tee Mills glared at him. "People like me? What's that supposed to mean? I came from the same place you did."

"Well, you sure as hell didn't want people to think so. You couldn't get soiled by association with the likes of me."

Tee Mills stalked around to the other side of the cart and leaned on it, staring down at the covered tray there. "Man, what do you know? Don't put words in my mouth. It was all different for you anyway."

"Different for me how? Just because I was honest about who I was? Do you actually think it was easy? Being shunned and ridiculed? Being dissed on a daily basis by somebody you thought was your closest friend—the only somebody you had ever—" Alvin caught himself. He turned away and inhaled deeply, trying to calm himself. He shook his hands out and centered himself.

"Look, I apologize," he said, making a study of the cart. "I had no right to come in and dredge up all that old bullshit. We were kids; it was a lifetime ago, like you've said. It's childish to keep harping on it. I'm just going to go. Again, sorry for all this."

He headed for the door. Behind him he heard Tee Mills lift the cover from the dish on the cart.

"Is this one of your recipes?" he asked.

Alvin came to a stop.

"When I called down, I specifically asked that they send me a vegan dessert. So I thought it might have been one of your recipes. Your place had really good desserts."

Alvin spun around. "What?"

"Vegtouffée. Your restaurant. I came by there once, you know."

"How do you know about my restaurant?"

Tee Mills' expression was guarded, his eyes soft. "I know a lot about you, Alvin. I kept track of you over the years."

Alvin didn't know what to say. It would've been enough to know that someone as famous and as busy as Tee Mills was had kept an eye on him, even visited his little restaurant that had barely lasted two years. But to know that Timothy Miller, his Tim, had watched him all this time made it even harder to comprehend. All this time, had Tim been thinking about him too?

Tim straightened and pulled his robe closed. He wheeled the cart out of the bedroom and parked it by the table Alvin had suggested when he first arrived. He grabbed the bottle of champagne.

"So would you reconsider?" Tim asked. "About having a glass with me? Look, I'm sorry about earlier, about being so bold. I was thinking that usually— Well, I don't know what I was thinking. I guess I wasn't sure of how you'd react. Even though seeing you now feels like we never had any real space between us, I know it's been a long time. And I didn't want to lose my nerve. So I was overcompensating a little, I guess. I thought I had to shoot my shot when I had the chance."

He poured two glasses of champagne and gestured toward the couch.

"Maybe we could just talk? As two old friends?"

Everything logical in his brain, every instinct of protection Alvin had in his body screamed at him to politely decline and leave, get out of that hotel room. But he couldn't force himself to move. Every part of him might have been telling him no, but that small portion of his heart which had never forgotten told him to stay, insisted he give it a chance.

He shrugged. "I think my shift ended about ten minutes ago, technically. So why not?"

Tim nodded and smiled.

"So you really came to Vegtouffée?" Alvin asked as he settled onto the couch and took the drink from Tim.

"Yeah. I mean, I'm not gonna forget a name like that, right? Vegtouffée?"

Alvin couldn't help but break into a smile. "Oh, okay. So you got jokes, huh?"

"Bruh, what was that about?"

Alvin smiled. "Listen, I was trying to give a feeling, a vibe. You know, like vegan but with a Deep South flair."

They both burst out laughing.

"Okay, okay," Alvin relented. "It was a pretty terrible name, I admit it. I can't believe I didn't hear about your visit though. We didn't exactly get a lot of famous customers."

"It was a weird time of day, I think. I'd had a show the night before and, of course, had woken up really late. So by the time I got there it was like mid-afternoon—on a Monday, I think—and it was pretty slow."

"Yeah, that tracks. It was always pretty slow."

"I asked for you, but they said you were off that day. And," he continued with a chuckle, "the server didn't seem to have a clue who I was."

"Which server?"

"She had pink dreads, I think?"

"Ah, okay, yeah. Rainbow-Lèa. If you had been India Arie or Cree Summer maybe she would have recognized you, but she definitely had a very specific vibe."

"*Rainbow-Lèa,* though?"

"I know. Don't even go there."

They chuckled and took another sip of champagne.

"It was a really nice spot, though," said Tim, "and the food was great."

"Thank you."

"Why did you give it up?"

"I don't know. I couldn't sustain it. Maybe it was the economy. Maybe Atlanta wasn't ready for Deep South vegan yet. Maybe it was the name. Maybe my heart just wasn't in it."

"But I thought you loved cooking. It seems like all you ever did in California."

Alvin studied him, a slightly amused expression on his face. "Wow. You really were stalking me, huh?"

Tim took a long sip and winked at him. "Blame it on social media," he said. "You post a lot. Not my fault if I happen to pay attention."

"But we're not friends on any social media apps." Alvin narrowed his eyes.

"Come on, son. You've never heard of fake accounts? Finstas? Alternate handles on Twitter?"

"So you mean we're friends and I just don't know it? That's a little sneaky."

"Shit, I'm world-famous, bruh. It comes with the territory. I can't have all the groupies on my jock."

Alvin groaned loudly and then laughed. "Okay, I'm going to need a lot more champagne if that's the kind of bullshit I'm going to be listening to."

Tim laughed and reached for the bottle and refilled Alvin's glass. "As long as you stick around, you can have as much champagne as you want."

"Well, in that case, I might not be here long," said Alvin, tongue firmly in cheek. "That bottle's almost done."

"Oh, we can get another—as many as you want. Remember, I'm not only world-famous but I'm rich as fuck too."

Alvin couldn't help but laugh. "And, yes. To answer your earlier question. Yes, that dessert is my recipe. Chef Matt is great, but his vegan repertoire is sadly lacking. So I gave him a couple of my better recipes—not my best, mind you, I have to keep something for myself."

"Of course," said Tim. "And good reminder."

He hopped up and jogged to the cart. He grabbed up the dessert from its tray, along with two forks. He flopped back down and placed it on the cushion between them.

"Can't let this go to waste. I love chocolate too much."

"So do I," agreed Alvin.

"And it's technically tomorrow by now and tomorrow's my cheat day, no matter what Angie says." He winked. "So I'm allowed to indulge in anything I want."

Alvin felt the blood rush to his face, and distracted himself with another forkful of dessert. Tim did the same and they were both silent for a moment, savoring the taste.

"Damn, that's good," said Tim finally. "You are talented."

Alvin smiled and nodded his thanks. They both had another bite. "So does that usually work?" he asked after a moment.

"What?"

"That stunt you pulled earlier. Answering the door with your robe open to your navel, with nothing on underneath except your freshly lotioned skin?"

"Oh, so you noticed then?" Tim was biting his lip again.

"You just spring yourself on unsuspecting bellhops or room service attendants? Half-naked and smelling good, and that's all it takes?"

Tim smirked and took another bite of dessert before answering. "I mean, honestly? Yeah. That's usually all it takes."

Alvin chuckled. "I bet. It's hard to resist the sexy famous singer for most people, I imagine." Tim raised a brow. "And that down-low shit is a turn-on for a lot of guys. Taboo, secretive, whatever."

"Well, it clearly isn't a turn-on for you, we have learned," said Tim. "I really didn't mean to piss you off like that."

Alvin waved it away. "It must have been hard all these years though. Living like that. Keeping a secret. It must have been lonely."

Tim frowned. "How many openly gay R&B singers do you know?"

"Well, there's a couple."

"Sure. But how many hits do they have? How famous are they? And you know the world was not the same place when you and I were fresh out of high school. I wanted a career, so I did what I had to do to get it."

"You always did have that drive."

Tim shrugged. "It wasn't the ideal situation. It weighed on me pretty heavy—always has. But it wasn't always lonely. And it wasn't always on-the-low hookups. Sometimes I could make a relationship out of it—or at least what I told myself was a relationship." His eyes widened and he took a gulp of champagne. "A couple of times, it was almost out of my hands. Some news items broke and almost caused some serious shit. I was seen at the wrong place too many times. And there was the one dude I was dating for a while— Well, that was a mess."

"Do you mean that stylist?"

"Yeah, Freddie Newsome. You heard about that?"

"Bruh," said Alvin, imitating Tim's earlier cadence, "the whole gay world heard about that."

Tim shook his head. "Man, do you know how much money we had to pay him off to squash that? He was hurt, I could tell. And it hurt me too, honestly. I think he just wanted me back, he wanted me to claim him. But I couldn't go there. I wasn't ready.

And to be completely honest I don't think I was really in love with him. Not like I was with—"

"Not like you were with?" asked Alvin.

Tim turned away. "Just not how I imagined it would feel, I guess."

Alvin could strongly identify with how the situation might have felt. He had a sudden tenderness for both Tim and his ex, Freddie; it couldn't have been easy trying to make something work with that kind of pressure.

Tim sighed. "Anyway, it was lucky it didn't make the headlines on too many big news fronts. The only one who had all the details correct was *The Shady Corner*, and people think they're too ratchet to be reputable."

Alvin dropped his fork and burst out laughing. The laughter just kept rolling and rolling. The emotional tension had built up since he'd entered the room and this was the release he needed.

Tim gave him a confused look. "What's so funny?"

"I'm sorry, I'm sorry. But *The Shady Corner*?" Alvin burst out laughing again. "It's just that I have this friend who swears by them for all his news. We always give him a hard time, but he just knew that—"Alvin caught himself. "I mean, he swears he always has the gossip before anybody else and we give him a hard time about it. But it seems like maybe he has the best source of all."

"I guess so," agreed Tim, his voice somber.

He rose from the couch and went over to the cart where he stood for a moment, silent. "I was scared that time." His voice was heavy when he finally spoke. "It seemed like everything was going to come apart. And then how I left Freddie—he was messed-up, I could tell. I wasn't sure if all of this—if any of this—was worth it anymore." He turned, leaning against the cart, and looked at Alvin. "Sometimes it feels like I've been scared forever."

Alvin felt a pang in his chest; Tim seemed to be hiding so much pain.

"I understand," said Alvin, "it is scary."

"But you were always so much braver than me."

Alvin shook his head. "No, I wasn't. I wasn't brave. People say that but it's not really true. Not for me."

"Coming out as a teenager—when you did, where we were from—that was brave."

Alvin shrugged. "Some of us—well, some of us don't really have the choice but to be 'out.' See, even if I wasn't gay, I never would have been one of the boys. I never would have fit in. I had different interests, I was *weird*. I was never going to be the masculine ideal. So when people assumed that made me gay, even though, of course, that wasn't what made me gay, it just made it doubly hard to deny or pretend. I could have forced myself into the role, like so many other people, but, for me, it would have meant destroying everything that I was inside. Not just a part, but everything. I never fit the bill of what a boy was supposed to be, and it would have crushed me."

He paused, thinking back, and took a deep breath. "Believe me, I know. I tried later, in college. And it almost erased everything about who I was. Luckily, I was older then, and I had enough perspective to reclaim myself after. But, for a moment there, I almost lost myself entirely. I dunno. Maybe fifty years ago, I would have done something else—been a priest, or become part of the church and hidden away there. Maybe end up being one of those sleazy shady deacons who is always looking at the tenor section with a little too much interest. But that kind of life seemed lonelier than being alone."

Tim was watching him intently as he spoke. Alvin could tell there was something burning inside of him to say, but he didn't want to press—not yet.

"At least your parents were cool."

Alvin gave a slight nod and looked toward the window. "Yeah, now they are. When I first came out as a kid my dad just shook his head and said how disappointed in me he was. It took him over a decade to even acknowledge that part of my life. And my mom was okay with it, or so she insisted. But every time anyone casually asked how I was doing, or if I had a girlfriend, she dipped in to talk over me so quickly, I'm surprised her tongue didn't twist into knots.

"Don't get me wrong. I'm lucky, and I know it. I'm lucky they didn't kick me out into the streets or disown me. I'm lucky and grateful. Still, to know that your parents are constantly on full alert, worried what the neighbors might think if too many of them found out; to sit up in church and know that they're tense the whole time wondering if somebody is going to sermonize about something that might have people looking under their lashes at me. To feel like you are an embarrassment to your family—even if they still love you—that fucks with your head. Sometimes I wish I had waited and just tried to play along, to have saved some of those awkward years. Maybe if I had lied, things wouldn't have been so tense, so stalled."

Tim came over and sat on the arm of the couch, seemingly deep in thought. "It didn't look that way from the outside. The way you describe. It seemed like your parents and you got along fine. Sometimes I almost thought you seemed smug in how easy things were for you."

"'Easy'?" Alvin was surprised. "It wasn't as hard as it could have been, but it didn't feel easy." Still Alvin knew that his situation must have been light years away from the home-life Tim had. "Is that why you hated me so much back then?"

Tim gave him a wild look, and slid down onto the couch, almost as if he'd been pushed.

"Hate you? Is that what you thought? That's crazy; I didn't hate you back then. I was jealous of you."

"Jealous? But you were the track star, Mister Popular, every girl wanted to be at your side. And you were jealous of me? How is that possible?"

"Yes, jealous. Even being young, in that school, with all those knuckleheads, you were brave enough to be yourself. Do you know how much I envied you? You say you didn't have a choice, and maybe not. But you didn't even try to find a disguise; you were completely yourself."

"And it cost me. A lot." Though he tried, Alvin couldn't hide the bitterness in his voice.

"I know," said Tim. "I'm sorry I—"

"No, I didn't mean that." Alvin sighed. "I don't know what I mean. I just know that it cost me a lot of heartache and pain."

Tim stretched his arm across the back of the couch and his fingertip touched Alvin's shoulder gently. "At least you didn't end up like me," he said.

Alvin saw the depth of pain in his eyes. Tim hadn't escaped his youth any more unscathed than Alvin had. His scars were just different.

"A lot of people would give up everything to end up like you."

Tim shook his head. "No, they wouldn't. Not if they knew."

He moved closer to Alvin until their shoulders touched, and he leaned against him. They sat for a moment, neither of them saying anything, the only sound, that of their breathing.

"So you really didn't know back then?" asked Tim, staring out of the same window Alvin had before.

"Know? That you were gay too?"

Tim dropped his head. "Yeah, that, I guess. But, more than that.... You didn't realize?"

"Realize what?"

Tim leaned back and stared at Alvin until Alvin felt compelled to turn and meet his gaze. Tim's eyes were warm, deep, and Alvin thought he could sit like this forever if Tim continued to look at him like that.

"Didn't you realize how much I liked you?" asked Tim.

Alvin's tongue suddenly felt frozen. He was scared to speak. A sudden rush of emotion came up, like a tidal wave within him, and hit a dam at the back of his throat. If he spoke, he knew, it would all come flooding out—all those years of wishing and hoping, the pining away he'd done for this man who had been the boy he'd thought about every day of his young years. It seemed as if he had wanted to hear those words ever since he could remember. He couldn't be trusted to handle them now, not rationally, not like an adult should; he was not in a rational state of mind.

He jerked his eyes away from Tim's gaze and stared straight ahead. He shook his head, unable to even say no.

"You don't remember that day?" asked Tim. "Right before Christmas break of our senior year?"

Are you fucking kidding me? Alvin wanted to scream at him. *Of course I remember that day. It meant everything to me. I was floating on air for the next two weeks before winter vacation ended, day and night; I couldn't believe it had happened. I sat by the phone, waiting and waiting and waiting for you to call. Checking my email every hour, hoping you would say something. Anything!*

But he said nothing, he just gave Tim a quizzical look.

"The snow day," Tim reminded him. "You have to remember that. Don't you?"

Alvin clasped his hands together. He wasn't sure he wanted to relive this; it hurt too much.

"'The snow day'? I remember everybody was so shocked and excited we might actually have snow for Christmas in Atlanta. Like it was a good omen or something. But I don't really remember what else happened that day. I just remember that after winter break you stopped communicating with me altogether."

Tim dropped his chin to his chest and his shoulders slumped. "I didn't handle it well," he admitted. "But I wasn't sure. I didn't know what to do. After that afternoon, my head was so messed up, just muddled. I didn't hear anything from you over break, and I was confused. Confused about what I felt. And confused about what you felt too. I thought maybe—I don't know—that maybe you didn't want to hear from me. Especially after you had asked me to come to your place and then—"

"Asked you?" interrupted Alvin. "You practically begged me to come to my place. You said you didn't want to go back to your house because your uncle was staying there with y'all. And you hated him."

The corner of Tim's mouth turned up a bit.

"I thought you said you didn't remember what happened that day?"

Alvin blushed and turned away.

"Anyway," continued Tim. "That was just an excuse. I never really hated my uncle, I was just scared of him."

"Scared of him?" Alvin's defenses went up and he stared at Tim with concern. The thought of anyone harming a young Tim made him instantly upset and ready to fight. "Did he hurt you?"

Tim noticed his concern, and, smiling, put his hand on Alvin's shoulder. "No, no, nothing like that. Don't worry. He would never do anything like that." Tim sighed deeply. "You know he was my mother's brother, right? And he came to stay with us after my dad passed. He and my dad didn't really get along because my uncle was gay—and he didn't hide it. So I hadn't seen him very much as a kid. But after my dad passed, he broke up with his boyfriend and my mom invited him to come stay with us for a little bit. Which turned into quite a while.

"I guess being around him reminded me too much of my dad. My dad was really vocal about his dislike for *faggots* and that kind of thing. Whenever the subject of my uncle came up, he would go on and on with my mom. And when she would say that she was the only sibling her brother had because the rest had disowned him, my dad would just say, 'Good. That's the way it should be. If my brother or anybody in my family was a faggot, I'd disown them too.' So needless to say, I didn't want to associate with him that much."

Alvin nodded.

"It just bothered me to be around him with other people. You know how it is, we would go to a cookout or family functions and he would be *The Gay Uncle*."

Alvin had to chuckle. "Yes, there's always one."

"Exactly. And nobody ever confronted him or anything but you could tell they were looking at him funny. Sometimes whispering behind his back and whatnot. I didn't want them doing that about me." He sighed. "Who knows? Maybe they weren't talking bad about him, maybe they just liked him. I dunno. It was stupid, how I acted then. But I was a dumb kid. And I was scared, somehow, that I'd be guilty by association. Does that make any sense?"

He looked at Alvin pointedly.

"Yeah," said Alvin. "I get it."

"Anyway, he was a really good dude," Tim continued. "Even after he moved out, he kept in touch with me. We've stayed close. He's really like the closest thing I have to a father figure." He paused for a moment. "And even though I've never told him, I think he knows. About me, I mean. I think he can tell, on some level."

"Those who care about us and really pay attention usually can."

Tim nodded.

"You'll come to it in your time," Alvin assured him. "You'll tell him when you're ready."

Tim sat forward suddenly, his hand on Alvin's knee. "When will I be ready?" he asked, his voice rough. "When will it be time? I'm getting old, it's all slipping away. I don't want to miss my shot again."

Again? The word rang out in Alvin's head.

"You're still young. You've got time. And you'll know when—you'll just know, you'll feel it."

"Just feel it, huh?" Tim's grip on Alvin's knee tightened.

"Yes." Alvin cleared his throat. He stood. "I don't know about you but I need a real drink. Let's see what y'all get in these fancy suite mini-bars." Alvin walked over to the mini-fridge and peered inside. "Bacardi? Ugh."

"I'll take the Scotch if you don't want it," said Tim. "Or the bourbon, whichever."

Alvin grabbed one of each. He tossed a bottle to Tim. "No ice."

"Don't worry." Tim winked as he caught the bottle. "Take it to the head, Alvin. Straight, no chaser. Don't be a punk."

"Oh, I'm good, playboy. This punk can handle his liquor, don't worry."

As Alvin approached the couch, Tim stood, holding out his tiny bottle. "Cheers."

"Cheers," Alvin answered, and they both knocked back their respective mini-bottles in one gulp.

Tim sucked air in through his teeth, let out a little whoop, and started moving his arms and torso in rhythm.

Alvin laughed. "What are you doing?"

"The choreography we memorized!" Tim exclaimed. He dashed around the couch and began to dance with more fervor. "From the snow day afternoon. Don't think I forgot–you don't get to change the subject that easily."

Alvin rolled his eyes, not wanting to go back to that, but the sight of Tim dancing in his robe, which threatened to fall completely open at any moment, combined with all the champagne and booze, made him giddy and he felt too warm to argue.

He recognized a few dance moves and it all came back to him. "Oh shit!" he yelped. "That was the day Mikkie Fiyah debuted his new song on *106 & Park*!"

"Yep," said Tim, giving a little pop-and-lock shoulder move. "And we were determined to learn the choreography immediately."

"Yes, I DVR'ed and we kept rewinding."

Tim danced up close to him, tugging at his suit jacket. "Come on, now, I know you remember some of those moves."

Alvin shook his head, but within seconds, he was joining in. He shed his jacket and they danced for a few minutes, Tim singing the song from their youth.

After a while, Alvin was waving his hands and flopped onto the couch, laughing. "Time out," he cried, between deep breaths. "I don't do this shit for a living like you, I'm getting old."

Tim, laughing, flopped down beside him. "Whatever, old man! You still got those moves, I see you."

Alvin laughed as he undid the top button of his shirt to cool down.

"Man, I remember all the girls in the audience screaming for him," said Tim. "They thought he was so fly."

Alvin sucked his teeth and raised one shoulder. "I mean, he was cute and all but the one I was watching the whole time was the—"

"Background dancer on the left!" Tim joined him in unison. They laughed.

"Yes." Tim gave Alvin a playful shove. "He was hot. With his little gap in his teeth and his skinny legs. He kinda reminded me of you, to be honest."

Alvin tried to hide his giddy reaction to that. "Whatever. I wonder what happened to Mikkie anyway. He hasn't had a song in years."

"He became a producer and behind-the-scenes guy," said Tim. "But he had a bad drug problem. Last time I ran into him at a studio session, he was pretty bad off. I tried not to think about what he used to be."

"I'm glad you never went that route. You hear all kinds of stories about the music industry."

"No, those weren't the demons I had to battle." Tim sidled up to him.

"You could've been a dancer back then too. I remember you in that purple ankh T-shirt and all those wooden bracelets you used to love. You looked like you could have been in a music video."

Alvin was taken aback. "You remember that?"

"I remember every detail about that afternoon. I'll never forget it." He moved closer to Alvin, pressing against him, the robe falling open a bit more and exposing the glistening skin of his chest. "It was my first real kiss." He stared into Alvin's eyes and bit his lip.

"You had girlfriends," said Alvin, narrowing his eyes and trying to fight the urges welling up within him. "I know you kissed them."

Tim nodded lightly, and ran his tongue along his lips. "But those weren't real kisses. They never made me feel like I felt when I kissed you. When I kissed you, I knew who I was, what I was."

"One kiss did all that?"

Tim slid even closer, putting his arm around Alvin's shoulders. "It wasn't just one kiss, Alvin. We spent the rest of the afternoon on your bed kissing and touching and exploring one another. Or did you forget that too?"

Alvin shook his head, he could feel his body going slack. "No, I never forgot."

Tim leaned in, his face inches from Alvin's. Just then something slid down the chain around Tim's neck, falling from around his collar where it had been nestled. The chain bounced a bit as the round object came to a rest. Alvin felt the breath hitch in his chest as he reached for the chain and lifted the ornament to examine it. *Could it really be?*

He turned the polished wooden ring around, examining it. There, on the curve was the carved letter *A*, with a diamond shape flanking it on each side, just as he remembered.

"This is the ring I made in shop class," he said, his voice feeling weirdly disconnected from his body. "In eighth grade."

Tim nodded.

"Patrick Simon said it looked stupid and gay, and I was embarrassed about it."

"But I told you I thought it was cool."

"So I pushed it in your hand and told you that you could have it then."

Tim nodded again, and clasped the ring between his forefinger and thumb, his fingers brushing Alvin's.

"And you kept it all this time?"

"Yes," said Tim. "I always wear it. Unless I have to take it off for a shoot or filming or something. But otherwise, it's always here, around my neck."

Alvin swallowed hard against the lump forming in his throat. "But why?" he asked, his voice full of disbelief.

"Because it reminds me of you. And because I think—no, if I'm going to say this, I have to say it. Not think, I know. Because I know I've been in love with you since you gave it to me. Even in eighth grade, even in high school. I've been in love with you ever since we first met, even before I could put a name to it."

Alvin felt tears sting his eyes. "So why didn't you call me? Why did I never hear back from you after that snow day? The whole last semester of school, graduation, prom, everything, and you avoided me like I had the plague. I thought you hated me."

"Because I was afraid. I told you. I've always been afraid. You said earlier that pretending to be someone who you weren't would have destroyed you. Well, back then, being who I really was would have destroyed me. I couldn't have handled it. And you reminded me of that every time I looked at you. When I saw you in the halls, when I caught a glimpse of you at a pep rally, it felt like my heart was turning in on itself. Like it might explode or disintegrate. And it was so strong that I knew if I ever admitted it, I would crumble into a thousand pieces."

Alvin watched as Tim's eyes seemed to drink in every detail of his face, the curve of his lips, the shape of his eyes, the small lines that formed at the corners of his mouth as he smiled.

"My love for you would have obliterated everything else. Nothing else would have mattered. And I wasn't strong enough to handle that then."

Alvin ran his hand along the side of Tim's face, tracing his jawline, feeling the roughness of the new stubble there. He traced his bottom lip with his finger. "And now?"

"Now I am strong enough."

"Are you sure?"

"Earlier you said I'll know when, I'll just feel it. I felt it today when I saw you again; I *knew* it. But the fear swept over me when I came out and there you were—in the flesh, real and breathing. Not just a memory, or a smiling picture on social media. I could feel you across the room; I knew every inch of you like I had seen you just yesterday. And I freaked out. The fear overtook me. I ran back into my hiding place of being aloof.

"And as soon as you'd walked out of the door, I was sick. I thought I might vomit. I wanted to run after you or throw myself out the window or something. I realized I'd made the biggest mistake of my life letting you just walk out of that door. I couldn't think straight all afternoon. I told myself I wasn't going to let you get away this time. I wasn't going to let that happen. I couldn't. Not again."

"And what if I hadn't been the one to bring up your order tonight? What if I decided I didn't want to come back up here again after this afternoon?"

Tim rested his forehead against Alvin's. "Why do you think I booked myself here all week? It wasn't just for a holiday visit."

"You were really gonna spend your Christmastime pursuing me?"

"If that's what it took. I wanted to give myself as many chances as I could. And I'll extend my stay another week or another month or more if I have to. I'm not prepared to leave Atlanta this time without letting you know exactly how I feel. I might not be strong enough or brave enough to get every step right, but I am strong enough and brave enough to let you know this is it; this is me; this is how I feel about you."

A rush came over Alvin, a rush that he had not felt in years, a rush, he realized, he had maybe never felt his entire adulthood. Something flared up within him, and in some way, somehow, he felt alive again. As if he had been waiting, stuck in a stasis half of his life, waiting for just this moment.

Still, somewhere a voice told him to be hesitant. Wasn't it just hours ago that Tim had been crippled by his fears yet again? How would he react if his manager knew, if his recording company knew, if the world knew the truth of who he was? Would he retreat again? Would he cut Alvin off just like he had when they were young?

Alvin had no answers. He was unsure. He was afraid. And still.

He put a hand on Tim's neck and pulled him close. They kissed. Tim was hesitant at first, but then moved with greater passion. Alvin was aggressive, demanding, drinking Tim in, as if he were determined to pull him in and never let him free of the feeling. His heart was once again in his childhood bedroom, just like that afternoon so many years ago, as the snow fell gently outside, only this time he was determined to stake his claim, make sure his passion was known and not soon forgotten.

Tim pulled away; he stood and held out his hand to Alvin who took it. Tim led him into the bedroom and stood at the end of the bed.

"Strip for me," he said, his voice husky.

"What?"

"I want to see your body."

Alvin was hesitant. When he was young, he had been so self-conscious about his body. He had done a lot of work to feel better about it, and had gained a new sense of confidence, still, here, standing before the man of so many fantasies, all that old self-doubt came flooding back.

Tim seemed to sense his hesitancy. "Would it help if I went first?" he asked.

Without waiting for a reply, he reached down and undid the belt of his robe, letting it fall open. He moved it off of his shoulders and it fell in a pile around his feet. His erection stood at full attention, and he slowly slid his hand down the shaft, his fingertips caressing the foreskin, before he let it bounce back, slapping against his stomach.

Perfection, thought Alvin. "I think that made it worse," he said, with a coy half-smile. "How am I supposed to compete with all of that?"

Tim smiled and shook his head. "You never realized how fine you were even back then. Don't you know when you would pass me in the hall and look back and find me stone-faced staring at you that it was all I could think about? I wanted to know what was under those clothes; I imagined how you looked, what your skin felt like, how fat that ass was exactly."

Alvin dipped his head. His skin felt flushed and prickly from Tim's attention. His own erection was growing quite noticeably in his slacks.

"So show me," Tim said, his voice a low rumble. He caressed his swollen cock. "Show me what I've been missing out on. What I've been imagining all these years."

Alvin pulled up on his shirt, untucking it from his pants.

"And take your time," added Tim, biting his lip. "I want to savor this."

Alvin lifted his chin, fighting not to show the exhilaration radiating through him.

He wore a lot more than just a robe, but he took his time unbuttoning the shirt, slipping off the undershirt, undoing and pushing down his slacks, pausing as he worked the material over his thighs and turning to the side in the process so that Tim could see just how fat the ass was exactly. He tossed his socks to the side and stood in his briefs.

He felt on fire watching the way Tim's gaze moved over his body, lapping up every inch like a thirsty cat with his cream. Alvin massaged his swollen cock through the fabric of his briefs, which seemed to focus Tim's attention

He looked up at Alvin, his gaze somewhat pleading.

"You said to take it slow," Alvin reminded him.

Tim bit his lips and spread his hand across his chest to caress his nipples. "Not too slow," he said with a catch in his voice.

Alvin nodded and pushed the briefs down to his feet, stepping out of them. He stood there, his body on full display, and reached down, pressing his hard dick against his stomach with one hand and caressing his balls with the other.

Tim inhaled deeply and approached him. He pressed himself against Alvin, grabbing his ass and pulled him close. He began to grind his hips and their hard cocks rubbed against one another. Alvin thought the sheer thrill of the friction might set them on fire.

As they kissed, Alvin ran his hands behind Tim's neck, drawing him close, crushing their chests together. Alvin could feel the ring on the chain pressing into his flesh and he broke away. Looking down, he lifted it, twirling it in his fingers, still in disbelief that Tim had kept it for so long.

Tim grabbed the hand in which he held the ring and brought it to his lips, kissing Alvin's fingers tenderly one by one, the ring slipping against his lips and then falling again to rest between his pecs.

Tim stepped back and gestured toward the bed.

"Lie down," he said, patting the foot of the mattress. "Put your head here."

Alvin climbed onto the bed, laying his head at the bottom with his fest resting against the pillows.

"Yes," he heard Tim hiss as he stood over Alvin.

He leaned forward and ran his hands up and down Alvin's torso. Then Tim put his knees on either side of Alvin's head and began to stretch himself over the length of his body. Alvin watched the planes of him as he moved. He watched his thick arms, the lines of his triceps cutting across the smooth luster of his skin; he studied the perfectly defined abs, the strong thighs, the thick cock dangling above, bouncing with every stretch and turn. Alvin ran his fingertips along Tim's midsection, his torso, anywhere he could touch. And then, when he was in position, Tim took him in his mouth.

A wave of sensation coursed over Alvin.

Tim dipped his head, taking all of Alvin, caressing the length with his tongue, his lips playing against the swollen head of his dick. Alvin reached up and positioned Tim's member so that he could return the favor, tasting him, salty, as he pressed against his tongue.

It was an overwhelming heady feeling as their mouths moved up and down one another's cocks. So many times Alvin had wondered what it might be like to touch him, to kiss him, to taste his skin. And throughout the years whenever Alvin had thought of a moment like this with Tim, he got a longing pang, a feeling of emptiness, as if some important part of him had been left somewhere, irretrievable. It was almost surreal now to be this close to him, to taste him, to smell him, to feel him. *Could it possibly be real?*

Alvin could sense that they were both close to finishing when Tim pulled away, rolling onto his side.

"Not yet," he pleaded. "I want this to last."

He gestured for Alvin to lie next to him, as he reached over his shoulder to retrieve a condom from the side table. Once Alvin was beside him, Tim pulled him close, wrapping his arms around his torso, his cock nestled between Alvin's ass cheeks. He turned Alvin's head to the side and leaned over his shoulder.

"I want to see your face."

He traced Alvin's lips with his fingers, his tongue following the path of his fingertips. He covered him with kisses, his neck, his shoulders, his back. Then he lifted one of Alvin's legs and crossed it over the other; wetting his fingers with his tongue, he prepared Alvin's entrance and positioned himself at the ready.

"Are you ready?" he whispered.

In response, Alvin only moaned and pressed himself back against Tim who took the cue and slowly pushed into him. Alvin gasped.

"I'll go slow, don't worry," Tim whispered against his neck, his kisses soft on his skin.

He pressed farther and soon Alvin was filled with him. He rocked his hips and Alvin let out a series of small moans.

"Is that okay?"

Alvin nodded. "It's so deep," he added, hardly able to speak.

Their lips locked and Tim began to thrust with more rhythm.

The seconds turned into minutes and then more, and Alvin lost all sense of time and place. All he knew was the cadence of their bodies moving together, filling and being filled, fingers intertwining, twisting the bedclothes in their grasp, clutching to keep themselves rooted so that they weren't lost forever to the pure ecstasy of their shared desire.

• • • •

AFTER, THEY LAY THERE, their limbs entwined, their breathing heavy.

"Déjà vu," whispered Tim, his eyes heavily lidded, as if he might drop off to sleep.

"What?"

"My song, *Déjà vu*. You know it."

"Of course. I remember it." His mind drifted back to the reception hall and the feeling hearing Tim's voice had evoked within him. "It's one of my favorites."

"Good," Tim replied, his eyes closed. "Because I wrote it about you."

Alvin didn't know how to respond. He was shocked. How many times had he sung along with that song? That song which he thought so encapsulated his own longing.

Tim, eyes still closed, pressed his mouth against Alvin's shoulder. "*And, baby, IIIIII will*," he half-sung half-murmured against his skin.

He nestled his face into Alvin's neck and fell asleep.

CHAPTER FOUR

No sunlight could make it around the high-end blackout drapes used in the presidential suite, but, still, come morning, the light had lightened enough that Alvin could make out Tim on the bed. He slept as Alvin ran his hand down his body, from elbow to ankle, letting his fingertips touch that delicious skin.

Alvin looked at him as his chest moved in and out. The man he had dreamt of all these years, there, beside him, to touch and to claim. He wondered if that were true. Would he truly be able to claim Tim now, or Tim claim him? Last night had been wonderful, magical, special, but would it continue? Was Tim strong enough and brave enough to take what they had discovered of one another outside the walls of this plush set of rooms. Alvin wasn't sure, but despite his misgivings, he let himself hope so.

At any rate, he had a shift to start in only a matter of hours. He gathered his clothes and dressed as best he could. He left a note under Tim's cell, lying on the side table, with his own phone number scribbled on it. It would be up to Tim now; he would let him lead the way. Alvin had wanted so much for so long that he could no longer carry the burden. If he heard from Tim again, he would be ecstatic; if not, he would do his best to move on with his life, wherever it led. He had worked too hard over the years to be okay with himself, he could no longer go back to that place of uncertainty.

In the bedroom doorway, he stole one last look at that beautiful body on the bedsheets, drinking in every detail.

He stole across the suite and left, closing the door behind him.

. . . .

SOMETHING HAD CHANGED, Alvin thought as he made his way down the hall. Inside the suite, he had told himself that he could no longer go back to that place of uncertainty. But it wasn't only about Tim he now realized. Looking around him, at the sterile walls of the hotel, he felt hemmed in, as if he wanted to break away and run as fast as his legs could carry him. Not because he was fleeing anything or afraid, but because he felt lighter, wide open, free. The walls of the hallway, the light color that he usually thought of as so refined, so elegant, now felt dingy and drab. Lifeless. He wanted color and sunshine and greenery. *Maybe,* he said to himself, *maybe it's time.* Time to turn in his name badge and give it another go. Tim had reminded him how much he had loved cooking, loved owning a restaurant. He'd once had a passion in life. Why had he let go of it? He'd taken a financial blow, sure. But he had recovered. What was stopping him now?

He reached the elevator.

What indeed?

As he got on, he felt his phone vibrate in his pocket, but he didn't check it as he always lost service when traveling between floors. But, as it approached the second floor, his phone went crazy. It began vibrating non-stop and he pulled it out, worried that it was malfunctioning or about to blow a fuse.

He swiped up and saw his general notifications. Tee Mills, his official accounts, were now following him on all his social media platforms. Alvin couldn't help but smile and shake his head but, still, he didn't think Tee following him would account for the fact that his phone continued to shake and hum.

He moved to his Twitter notifications which kept popping up more than most.

It was a tweet from Tee Mills himself. Not a direct message but a tweet, a public tweet, in which Alvin was tagged. A tweet for all three million of his followers to see. It was a heart emoji followed by a ring emoji and the words *I already miss you baby*.

Alvin was stunned. His eyes widened as the notifications multiplied, thousands upon thousands of people liking, retweeting, and commenting on the post. His phone froze and he was forced to reboot. How many people were seeing this, commenting on it, speculating, taking screenshots?

He stood staring at the front of his phone, his mouth agape.

"Getting off?" a voice asked him.

In front of him, impatient hotel guests waited to get on the now open elevator.

"Oh sorry," he said and scurried out.

He stepped aside, and stood there for a minute, shaking his head and grinning, trying to process what it all meant.

He looked down the corridor which led to the main lobby. There just near the door was the massive Christmas tree they had installed. One of many, they called this one the Silver Tree. All the ornaments and tinsel—everything on the tree—was silver and the pine needles were frosted with a light dusting of snow.

It shone like some great star there in the early morning light which came in through the front entrance. Alvin couldn't help but stare at it, fixated by its shimmer and promise of a beautiful holiday.

"Don't you see that mistletoe, we're gonna get to know each other better, cuz this is my Christmas..."

An enormous smile spread across his face as the song wafted from the speakers. This was his favorite Christmas song of all time, ever since he could remember. Whenever he heard that rich, warm voice singing of presents and cards and the world filled with cheer, he knew all was right. It was the warmth of the season he craved. And he remembered now listening to this very same song, that Christmas morning in his senior year, his heart full to bursting thinking back on the afternoon spent with Tim, dancing and kissing and knowing something meaningful had happened.

And here he was, having come full circle.

He needed some fresh air.

Alvin dipped into the dining room and headed for the employee break room. At the other end of the bar he spotted Davon who, luckily, did not see him. Davon was staring at his own cell phone, swiping as fast as he could, his eyes wide and his mouth twisted in surprise. Alvin grabbed his coat from the hanger and headed for the lobby, but as the door swung shut behind him, he heard one of those blasted jingle bells hung above ring out as it was jostled.

"Ohhh no!" Davon cried out behind him. "No, no! Bitch, you tried it! You better get back here and give me all the tea!"

Alvin picked up his pace and made it to the lobby where he dove behind the silver tree and tried to slink along the wall, hoping its glorious, shining branches would hide him from Davon's view as he made his escape. All the while he was chuckling.

Davon rounded the entryway and saw him. He grabbed first one then another plastic silver ornament and lobbed them at Alvin.

Full-on laughing by now, Alvin dodged the ornamental grenades and threw up his hands in mock surrender even as he kept his feet moving.

"I don't know what you're talking about, Davon," he said.

"You dirty, filthy strumpet! Don't you lie to me. It's all over *The Shady Corner* newsfeed already!"

"You know, you really shouldn't read that trash," admonished Alvin with a wink. He turned and sprinted for the front door. "Merry Christmas, Davon!"

"Come back here!" yelled Davon.

"I promise I'll call you later," Alvin called back. "But I gotta go!"

"Call me later? Why you scandalous slut! You better!"

Deniece came trotting into the lobby, running over from where she had been gossiping at the registration desk.

"What on earth are you doing, Davon? Why are you out here causing a scene?"

Davon spun around to respond and was smacked in the face by one of the silver angels hanging from a branch. He swatted it away. "Alvin was right," he muttered, "somebody is going to lose an eye." He gazed over at Deniece and stopped, stupefied. "Too bad I couldn't lose both of them."

"What if a client heard you?" asked Deniece. "Or Randall? And are those ornaments all over the place? Are you really out here acting this much of a fool?"

"Do not come for me, Rudolph the Red-Nosed Heifer. Especially not in that outfit!"

"What's wrong with my outfit now?"

"Nothing, I guess. But does Mrs. Claus know you raided her lingerie drawer?"

Deniece snatched the Santa cap from her head and threw it at Davon.

"This is a perfectly acceptable work outfit," she cried. "And don't change the subject. Who were you out here yelling at anyway?"

"I was yelling at Alvin's fast ass. That whore ran out of here like somebody had just posted his bail."

"So what?"

"So what? Heifer, keep up! He was coming from the presidential suite."

Deniece threw up her hands. "And?"

"And? And he was wearing the same clothes he had on yesterday! Or most of them, at least."

Deniece's jaw dropped.

Davon held up his hands and peered around the lobby. "Ladies and gentleman, she's up to speed," he announced.

"Shut up!" squealed Deniece. "So do you mean to tell me that Alvin—that he and Tee Mills were—that they...."

"Girl, here, just read about it before you lose all capacity for speech. It's all over social media." He handed her his phone.

"Social media?" She gasped as she pored over the screen.

As she scrolled through the news in shock, Davon studied himself in the darkened glass of the foyer wall. He ran a finger along his eyebrows.

"You think Jaz could squeeze me in this afternoon for a threading and a facial?" he asked. "What if *The Shady Corner* contacts me for a statement on all this mess? I am Alvin's best friend, after all."

Deniece gave him a look, one brow raised.

"*The Shady Corner* are not going to contact you, Davon."

"No? Oh, do you think this is TMZ-level tea?" He clapped his hands together. "Bitch, I might go viral!!"

Deniece rolled her eyes. "Don't hold your breath, sis."

"They might interview you too. After all, somebody will simply have to take a picture to commemorate that otherworldly, treacherous wardrobe."

"You know what, please do see to those raggedy brows of yours," Deniece replied as she continued to scroll the newsfeed. "And while you're at it, ask Miss Jaz if she can also adjust your funky attitude."

Davon snatched his phone from her, narrowing his eyes.

"Don't be salty. We all know you're just mad because I was right all along about Tee Mills. I told you—I *know* when somebody is family."

Deniece opened her mouth to retort but couldn't say anything.

"Uh huh, exactly. I didn't think so," said Davon wryly as he walked away.

Deniece shook her head and started gathering up the jettisoned ornaments. She was trying to fit them all back in an appropriate spot on the Silver Tree as a familiar song popped up in rotation overhead.

"Deliciously having a wondrous wintry time...."

She lifted her chin and listened to that dreaded song for a moment, smiling with a twinkle in her eye.

"Well," she said, looking at one of the small silver angels, "it looks like Alvin escaped just in time."

. . . .

OUTSIDE, IN THE PARKING lot, the air was crisp and chilly and Alvin pulled his jacket tight around him. The breeze was brisk but not yet cutting; it seemed like winter had staked its claim, after all. But he didn't mind the sudden drop in temperature. He felt warm inside, almost as if he were glowing. The sun was shining and he closed his eyes, smiling, lifting his face to its rays, and singing to himself.

"Don't you see that mistletoe, we're gonna get to know each other better, cuz this is my Christmas...."

His phone sprang back to life and buzzed again.

He opened up the new text message.

[TIM]
Sorry you had to rush out this morning
Was really hoping we could have breakfast together
Sad to wake up without you beside me
Hope you saw my message online

[ALVIN]
Sorry I had to run
Work stuff
Yes, I saw it

[TIM]
Good

**Now that the word's out, maybe we can have dinner
tonight?**
At the Solitary Heart? 8 o'clock?
I can pick you up
**There might be some paps, but if you don't mind, I
won't**
I'd really like to show you off to the whole world
(...)
(...)
(...)
Alvin?
Please say yes

Alvin gazed up at the hotel. Somehow, though he had not admitted it to himself until just this moment, he knew he wouldn't be coming back here for much longer. Not as an employee anyway. He was decided, he would hand in his notice today. Tomorrow, Christmas Eve, would be his last day at this place, in this life. The tether had snapped and he was set free. He didn't know where to, maybe California again, and he didn't know how or what. But he knew why. A new chapter was a new chapter. If he was ready to make a fresh beginning that meant facing his fears. Being strong enough and brave enough.

This was happening so fast, perhaps too fast. They had only reconnected less than a day ago, and here they were using words like "love" and saying how much they missed one another. Anyone with any good sense would tell him that this is not how you did things – you did not rush into love like this. But was it a rush? These feelings had been there, hidden away, sometimes shoved away, ever since he could remember. And so had they been for Tim as well, judging by his confession the night before.

What would it mean to be with this man? Especially in this scenario—him fresh out of the closet, living a life in the public eye. Alvin's feelings might not have changed in all this time but this man had most certainly changed. Alvin wouldn't just be dating Timothy Miller, he'd be dating Tee Mills, the world-famous singer. Was he prepared for that level of scrutiny? This would be love under a microscope, with everyone watching and waiting. What if he failed; what if they failed? Was giving his heart to Tim worth the peril of all that?

Was he truly ready for this?

His finger hovered over the phone as he contemplated a reply.

[TIM]
Alvin?

[ALVIN]
(...)
(...)
(...)
Yes
Yes, I'd love that.
8 o'clock sounds good.
I assume you already have my address, you stalker?

[TIM]
LOL Yeah, I got it.
See you then.
❤❤

Alvin smiled at the reply.

As he moved to get into his car, he felt something against his skin.

He lifted his chin, blinking, and held out his hand.

Snowflakes, small, soft, and wet, fell on his palm.

In Atlanta? Snow for Christmas?

Maybe it was a sign, an omen after all, he thought to himself, remembering that fateful snow day so long ago.

Humming to himself, he got into his car.

Things were going to be different, and he couldn't be happier about it.

COPYRIGHT

Don't miss out!

Visit the website below and you can sign up to receive emails whenever Lawrence I. Hill publishes a new book. There's no charge and no obligation.

https://books2read.com/r/B-A-LILJ-GJTIB

BOOKS 2 READ

Connecting independent readers to independent writers.

Did you love *Déjà Vu: A Short Romance*? Then you should read *That Summer in Spain*[1] by Lawrence I. Hill!

[2]

It wasn't just a role this time...

Xavier Duran is ready for the breakthrough film role of his career, and he thinks he's found it.

Not only does this new job take Xavier to the beautiful countryside of Spain, it also takes him right into the arms of his silver screen crush, Hollywood hunk, Dennis Herbert.

Dennis may be gorgeous but everyone knows he's straight. Or is he?

---

1. https://books2read.com/u/brVnWw

2. https://books2read.com/u/brVnWw

Lines blur and soon Xavier can't tell if Dennis is just playing his lover or if he wants to take on the role off-screen as well. And what about Dennis' beautiful model girlfriend?

Xavier has been burned before, and he isn't sure he wants to be the secret lover again. He's certainly not ready to risk his feelings on something deeper.

But passion presides and soon Xavier and Dennis are tangled in a web of fraught emotions and uncertain advances.

Is this only a fling? Or is this the beginning of a real romance?

One thing's for certain, it's going to be a scorcher of a summer.

Read more at https://www.facebook.com/lawhillwrites/.

Also by Lawrence I. Hill

That Summer in Spain
Déjà Vu: A Short Romance

About the Author

When Lawrence was a young boy, he watched the film '84 Charing Cross Road' over and over again and dreamed of living in a grubby little studio in NYC and writing books. He's finally got the grubby little studio in the city, and now on to the rest.

Read more at https://www.facebook.com/lawhillwrites/.

MOODY BOXFAN
BOOKS

About the Publisher

Moody Boxfan Books promotes storytelling for the lesser heard voices. Life is not seen through one pair of eyes, neither should our books be.